Humorous Erotica

First Time, Rough Swingers, Kinky Family, Eroctica

Short Stories for Women Daddy

Lana Kendra

Copyright © 2023 Lana Kendra

This is a work of fiction; names, characters, places, and incidents are either the product of the author's imagination or are used fictitiously, and any resemblance to actual people, living or dead, business establishments, events, or locales is entirely coincidental.

This e-book is for your personal use only and may not be resold or given to anyone else. If you want to give this book to someone else, please buy an extra copy for each person. If you're reading this book and didn't buy it, or if it wasn't bought for your personal use only, go back to your favorite ebook retailer and buy your copy. Thank you for acknowledging this author's efforts.

Table of Contents

Content Warning

Due to its sexual content, this book is only for those over the age of legal adulthood. There are some topics with a lot of foul language. All of the characters are at least eighteen years old.

Introduction

Are you in search of an exciting and thrilling book to read? Look no further than this extensive collection of Erotic Suspense book. I offer a wide range of genres, including Romantic Erotica, Fantasy, and Urban BDSM Fiction, to cater to even the most discerning reader. Whether you enjoy Anthologies, Westerns, or Paranormal Romance, I have something to suit your taste. My collection also includes Poetic Folklore, Interracial, Black & African American Literary Criticism, and Gothic Horror for those who crave a deeper and darker reading experience. If you're interested in Futuristic, LGBTQ+, Short Stories, or Lesbian literature, my diverse range of options will keep you captivated. Additionally, I offer Humorous, Victorian, New Adult, and College Women's Psychological Mysteries for those seeking a lighter but equally engaging read. Furthermore, My Fairy Tale Collections,

Transgender, Contemporary Western, Bisexual, and Poetry genres will transport you to different worlds and explore a variety of themes. For my Teen and Young Adult readers, I have a selection of European Geography, Cultures, eBooks, Loners, Outcasts, Mythology, Folk Tales, and much more. With such a wide array of options to choose from, you'll never run out of thrilling and enchanting stories to immerse yourself in.

This is a story of cute teens alone in the house and having good and quality time to themselves. Enjoy the sexual tentions embedded in this story.

It is important to emphasize that this content is exclusively intended for individuals who are 18 years of age or older.

Humorous Erotica

The folks Cassie and I were closest to left for the summer almost as soon as school let out, whether it was to travel to Lake Tahoe, Europe, or wherever else they wanted to see family or just to get away from it all and enjoy a true vacation. Although there were still individuals in the area, none of our old pals were there.

It was very unfortunate. This summer was our final one before we left for college. We're both attending State, which is a reputable university, and the in-state tuition is far less expensive than at many other universities.

Normally, we would also have left. Even though our parents both work in highly competitive fields—our dad is an architect and our mom is a realtor—they are able to handle part of their work from a laptop while on vacation. But Dad was working on a big project for an Italian company this summer. He needed to be in the office to work directly with his team on this, his first significant foreign project that may be a huge step forward for both his career and reputation. He was aware of our disappointment, but if all went well, he would take us to Italy while the construction was underway.

I was kind of trapped hanging out with my twin sister Cassie, trying to come up with anything to do. We could use Dad's car for day trips and to pick him up after work if one of us drove him to work every morning. However, it was too disjointed to feel like a true holiday.

When our next-door neighbors decided to take a two-week vacation in early July, they requested me to make sure everything was okay, including feeding the cats and changing the litter when needed. They also said I could use their pool whenever I wanted.

Mom advised us to just order pizza for dinner the following day because Dad was going to be working late and she was at a work/social function.

We were going to be hungry by late afternoon, I knew, but I still had to walk over next door and feed the cats. While I fed the kitties, I asked Cassie if she wanted to go. After she said okay, the two of us crossed over. The two cats ran in from the other room as soon as I opened the door and entered. I filled the water dish and the food dish for the cats. I looked in the trash can. It was one of those automated jobs that collected the waste and placed it in a bag for disposal approximately once every few days. My work was done because it wasn't filled yet.

I told Cassie about the pool and asked if she wanted to see it as we made our way back outside. She thought that sounded okay, so we headed to the backyard. A new pool, kidney-shaped in design, had lounge chairs surrounding it and a little fountain at one end that spewed water into the pool.

"Wow, Connor, that looks great. I'd love to hop in right now."

"We didn't bring our suits."

"So? Haven't you ever heard of skinny-dipping? I mean it's no big deal. It's just the two of us."

Nothing major? To me, it felt like a weird arrangement. I never would have considered making such a suggestion. Not to my sister, for sure.

However, now that she had made the suggestion... Was it truly my intention to be a stick in the mud about such a thing? I mean, that kind of behavior hardly raised an eyebrow these days. We also didn't have any towels, but I was aware that bringing it up would make me look completely ridiculous.

"Sure, okay, if you want to," I replied, my mind still reeling at the whole notion.

Great, she exclaimed.

It was already getting late in the day, and there were no lights on in the pool or surrounding it. That surprised me a little because I had been a little afraid I might look foolish.

With her back to me, Cassie was undoing her bra and taking off her top. Next, I witnessed her removing her shorts and subsequently her underwear. She turned to face me once more and proceeded to descend the steps into the pool until the water reached her chest, just above her nipples.

The truth is that Cassie and I were twins and spent our childhoods together. We used to communicate constantly, enjoy activities together, and be extremely close friends. However, there had never been any sexual activity between us. It happens frequently for brothers and sisters to "accidentally" (or even unintentionally) witness their sibling getting out of the shower or doing something else, but that never happened with us. Though I never really gave it much attention, I had seen her a few times in only her bra and underwear, which wasn't really any more revealing than seeing her at the pool in a bikini. I was aware of the guidelines.

I was having strange mental effects from watching her undress. Really, I'd always been able to brush that kind of thing off as inappropriate. It felt like we had that side of the problem covered because she and I were dating fairly frequently.

I mean, I knew this wasn't going to be a huge deal. People regularly go skinny dipping without getting into any kind of trouble. It was evident to me that I wasn't some sort of pervert who was infatuated with his sister. We were a nice, sitcom-loving American family.

"Hey, slowpoke! What's keeping you? Come on in. The water feels great."

I took my shorts off and my T-shirt off. I was a little anxious about removing my boxers, which was the following step. To prevent my dick from getting any notions, I was attempting some sort of mental workout, but I knew it wouldn't last long. Moving quickly, taking off my boxers, and diving into the pool as soon as possible was my best course of action.

Still, as I descended the pool's steps, I felt my dick beginning to protrude. Luckily, I was only in the water up to my chest rather than reaching the fully exposed stage.

Yes, Cassie was right—the water felt wonderful. You got the impression that the water and your body were one continuous surface because of the ideal temperature.

I turned to face Cassie, who appeared utterly content and at ease. It was too dark by now to make out her physique, or any specifics. Nevertheless, I felt this way. My twin sister and I were standing just a few feet apart, both fully nude, and I had the impression that there was some sort of sexual connection between our bodies because of the water.

Of course, I wasn't trying to feel any of this, but there was something about it that made me feel more attracted to someone than I had ever done before.

I had thought that my dick would drop once I was in the water, acclimated to the surroundings, and realized that this was just one of those "back to nature" situations, not one of those sicko "perving on my sister" situations. Still, it didn't. In no way. All I could think to myself was that I was relieved Cassie had not chosen to approach me or anything.

Cassie eventually said, "It's probably time for us to head home. Dad will probably be getting home soon."

She headed to where her clothes were after climbing the pool's steps. I couldn't stop gazing at her behind.

I seized the moment to quickly exit the pool before she turned around and saw my boner, because her back was still turned toward me.

I opted to forego my boxers and quickly put on my shorts since we didn't have a towel. After putting my boxers in a pocket, I reached for my T-shirt and put it on. Cassie may have taken the same action with regard to her underwear.

"It was quite pleasant," Cassie remarked. "I really love being in the water like that, especially in a private pool."

We made our way back to our home. Mom was still at whatever party she was attending that evening, and Dad hadn't returned yet. I let Cassie use the restroom and get dry first. She dressed in one of those long T-shirts that girls wear to bed, along with maybe some underwear.

After toweling myself dry, I changed into my summer uniform of a T-shirt and cotton running shorts and headed downstairs to the TV room. Already, Cassie had selected a sitcom to watch and placed an order for pizza. I took the pizza and a few dishes into the TV room with me when the delivery man showed up, along with a few bottles of water, so we could eat while watching TV.

After a short period, Dad entered. He was fine with the Chinese food his workplace colleagues had ordered for supper, but he was more than ready for a drink. After turning off the television, we went outside to greet him and find out about his day.

He was cheerful despite having had a demanding day at work. "It seems to be going really well. It's an exciting project and it's really interesting working on something where the culture and all the building codes and regulations are so different. I feel like I probably ought to take one of those new app-based language courses to fit in better."

He had his drink down and was prepared to go to bed. There was no way of knowing when Mom would return, as her primary purpose for attending these gatherings was to make as many connections as possible before the people she could speak with left.

Since Cassie and I were also somewhat exhausted, we made the decision to simply go to our rooms. I let her finish brushing her teeth before going to the restroom to urinate and clean my own teeth.

"Good night," I said to Cassie as I made my way to my bedroom.

Just as I was getting into bed, there was a knock on my door. When the door opened, Cassie poked her head inside. "Can I come in for just a second?"

"Sure, come on in."

Cassie entered the room. Her expression seemed a little unsure of the question she was going to pose. "Connor, I know this is weird of me to ask, but did you have...well, you know...a boner when we were in the pool together? I mean, I'm not trying to embarrass you, I don't know, I was just curious."

God, oh God. Was that really all she asked me? Truly? Aw sh*t.

"Cassie, I didn't mean to... I mean I didn't mean to embarrass you or anything. It just kind of happened. I'm sorry. I really didn't mean for that to happen. I know it wasn't right."

"Connor, you don't need to be embarrassed. Believe me, I don't want to embarrass you. I guess I was just trying to understand. I'm not passing any kind of judgment at all. Look, you're my brother and I love you, and I don't want you to feel embarrassed about anything. I mean I was just trying to figure out some things. You know, skinny-dipping isn't supposed to be any big deal or anything, right? People in California and lots of other places do it all the time. It's like it's not supposed to be sexual at all. So I was just curious. Did I do something wrong?"

"Cassie, you didn't do anything wrong. Nothing wrong at

all. It was all me. I mean you're my sister and so I know perfectly well I'm not supposed to think anything like that about you. And I thought it would go away, but there was something about being there in that warm water with you, with both of us naked, and it felt like the water was just connecting us or something. I don't know if that explains anything. It's probably just an excuse. But I am sorry about that."

"Connor, don't worry about it at all. I'm not offended. And you didn't do anything wrong at all. And yes, there is something about being in the water like that. I do understand what you're saying. And I did enjoy it. Thanks for inviting me."

Cassie went back to her room and shut the door to my bedroom. Even though I was still ashamed and extremely bewildered, I had no idea how to handle the situation. I eventually managed to nod off.

Neither Cassie nor I felt like waking up early the following morning to drive Dad to work. That meant that because Mom had another event that night and had spent the entire day attempting to sell houses, we were trapped without a car. However, since summer is generally a lazy season, we were content to simply hang out.

Cassie curled up with a book she had started after breakfast, and I made the decision to attempt organizing some of the mess in my room and closet. We assembled in the kitchen at midday to prepare sandwiches for lunch. After that, we spent some time hanging around, although we were both becoming a little restless. Cassie proposed that we go for a jog. I thought that sounded excellent, so we prepared ourselves and left.

We headed out to a park about a mile away, which was a pretty nice place to jog, and we completed a fairly leisurely five miles there. Thankfully, it wasn't too hot, but by the end, we were both practically saturated in perspiration.

"Connor, why don't we stop off and feed the cats on the way? That way we won't have to get dressed again to come over later," Cassie suggested before we left for home.

We swung by to feed the kitties since I had their house key on the same ring as ours. The cats didn't appear to mind if it was a little too early, but I wasn't sure. We were done because the litter box was still functional.

"Hey, can we go take a look at the pool again?" Cassie asked as we were leaving and I secured the front door.

I didn't think there was a unique purpose for us to make a second trip to view it later, as we had already fed the cats. We then strolled back towards the swimming pool.

"That looks so perfect. Do you want to hop in so we can rinse the sweat off and enjoy the pool?" Cassie asked, glancing at the swimming area.

Truly? once more? Did she not recall what had occurred the day before? And it was still daylight, not nightfall or dark, at this moment.

As I stood there trying to come up with anything to say, Cassie took off her tank top. This time, she was looking directly at me, and I was not averting my gaze. She undid her sports bra and threw it together with her shirt on the deck.

Despite my best efforts to act as though all of this was perfectly normal, I could feel my jaw dropping. I mean, I hadn't really had a chance to see Cassie's nipples and breasts until last night, and here they were in front of me. Like me, she was tall and slender, and her breasts complemented her figure. Perfect hemispheres, they jiggled just enough to make me crazy—not so huge as to be droopy, nor flat.

I was making an effort to act as though I wasn't staring or gawking. Her nipples were obviously perky, and I had the impression that they were protruding, but I couldn't be certain and was too shy to further investigate the matter.

After throwing away her socks and running shoes, Cassie took off her running shorts and put them in her pile of clothes. She then undid her underwear and placed it on top of the heap. Not like she was slow-teasing or anything, but she didn't have to. Still, I was captivated. Unlike my filthy blonde hair, Cassie's was dark brown, and when she undressed, I noticed a beautifully cut patch of wispy dark hair. Her bush and what little of her pussy I could see, or her breasts and nipples, I couldn't decide which attracted me more.

After placing her underwear on the laundry pile, she straightened up and said, "Hey Connor, what about you, slowpoke?"

I was going to have to strip in front of her, with her watching every move, as she wasn't going to the pool just yet. I couldn't attempt to turn around while she undressed, not after she'd allowed me to follow her entire nude transformation process.

I threw my running clothing on the porch after removing it. I took off my running shoes and socks after untying them. After that, I undid my running shorts and was left standing in my underwear. For a brief moment, I thought Cassie might proceed to the pool, but she remained in the same spot, waiting for the big reveal.

This was one strange circumstance. more so in light of yesterday. We kind of pretended yesterday that we weren't ogling one other's body, you know? She had now stripped off all of her clothes in front of me and was expecting me to reciprocate. In what way was this meant to be unrelated to sex? How could this be merely one of those nature-based activities that emphasizes simply being natural and such? When it came to my dick, there was absolutely nothing natural about this. However, what option did I have?

I undid my briefs and placed them on top of my other belongings. I was standing there with a major hard-on in front of my twin sister, totally nude.

Cassie was staring just as hard as I had while she was taking off her clothes. Her eyes widened even more at my protruding hard-on. It nearly made me question if we would actually enter the water or if we would simply stand there and gaze at one another.

I followed Cassie as she turned and proceeded towards the pool stairs after what seemed like an uncomfortably long period.

We stood in the pool together, feeling the cool water wipe away our perspiration, and we lingered for a few minutes, relishing in the feeling of the water around us.

Cassie turned to face me and said, "You know how you mentioned yesterday that you felt like you were naked and that we were connected by the water? I definitely feel that now. It is really sexy. I know it's not supposed to be, because we are twin brothers and sisters, but it's just the two of us. And it feels good, I don't know about you.

"I'm positive you had a great day yesterday, and I'm positive you're having one today as well. My nipples have been protruding since I removed my bra in front of you, and let's just say, other parts of me would be drenched even if we weren't in the pool, if that makes you feel any better. If you don't mind me telling you, you have a really attractive figure as well as a really attractive boner."

I did enjoy hearing her say all that, but it wasn't supposed to be me having a rock-hard boner for my sister, or her putting on a strip show for her brother, or talking about getting wet for him. Did I mind? What the hell? None of this was supposed to be happening.

Cassie was staring at me as though she was waiting for me to respond. "Connor, how about you? As far as I know, this is the first time you've ever seen me nude. At least not in broad daylight. Anything to add, then? I kind of expected you to say something along the lines of how impressed you were. sexy perhaps? How come you have nothing to say when we are both in the same pool, completely nude, and together? Oh my god! What is the matter with you? Do you handle your dates this way?"

There were so many restrictions against any part of this equation that I couldn't believe my twin sister was asking, more like demanding, that I tell her how hot she looks in her underwear.

"Cassie, you look incredible. Your physique is quite attractive. I suppose that I find it hard to accept that any of this is real. Furthermore, I'm not stating that I'm against this happening. You are very beautiful. All of you, your bush and breasts included—I suppose especially them."

When Cassie heard the last bit, she tried not to chuckle.

"You knew I had a boner yesterday, even though it was dark," I remarked. You're getting naked in front of me in broad daylight today, and it seems like my skull is going to blow up. You understand how I feel because you witnessed what was going on with my dick. Simply put, I'm not sure what to do with all of this. You realize that this isn't supposed to be occurring at all, after all."

Cassie remarked, "You know, Connor, maybe there's a reason why this all works out for us." Throughout high school, we both dated a wide range of people. However, I find that guys usually fit into one of two groups. One group consists of incredibly lovely guys that I like and enjoy hanging out with, but they are more like buddies to me. Therefore, if they want to kiss good night or whatever, it feels a little strange. You're aware?

I mean, I've made out with some of them, but I really don't want to do much of anything with somebody who just wants to brag about me to his friends. Especially in high school, where you know the word gets around to everyone.

"In the other category are guys who are usually hotter, but when they're out with me, I know the real point for them is going as far as they can with me, so they can brag to their friends about it when they get back to school next Monday. And it's weird, sometimes they can be kind of nice and fun for the first part of the date, and then suddenly something shifts and I feel that shift to where they're just a potential trophy for them.

"I guess the thing is that, even if it breaks all kinds of rules, I know I can trust you in a way I can't trust anyone else. It's probably different for you when you go out on dates."

Although Cassie's statement astonished me, I knew what she meant. "It's a little different for me," I responded. "There are some girls I like and enjoy talking with and stuff, but only as classmates or friends. And that can get a little awkward at times if they're hoping we can be more than friends. There are some other girls who like me and would probably be willing to do stuff with me, but I don't quite feel that way about them. At least not enough. I don't want to do something with them and have them feel like we're some big item or something. I guess there are some guys who don't care, but I don't want to end up hurting their feelings, so..."

Cassie remarked, "I understand that." "It makes a lot of sense. Perhaps that's what's so special about you and me— we love each other, we feel so linked, and we don't have any hidden agendas to use the other to impress our friends. Of course, we couldn't tell anyone about it anyway, given the circumstances.

Therefore, even though it may seem strange, being nude with you seems secure in a way that it wouldn't be with anyone else, even though everyone else would find it completely inappropriate. Are you able to understand that?"

Yes, what you're saying makes sense to me, even though it shouldn't, I said. I'm so happy we're together right now. Yes, it is enjoyable to be nude in the pool with you. In all honesty, I find it really amazing and very moving to watch you in your underwear."

After maintaining a conversational distance in the water, where one maintains a certain distance from another person without being too close, Cassie grinned and approached me, giving me a hug.

Thankfully, our serious conversation diverted my attention, and before long, I was feeling her breasts and nipples against my chest, though I wasn't sure how long that would last. Nevertheless, I couldn't help but remember that Cassie was my sister, and I kept reminding myself that what she was experiencing was our closeness, not some sort of forbidden lust.

I was able to keep my dick under control by reminding

myself of that.

This naked hug with Cassie was the sexiest thing that had ever happened to me in my life—I mean, I had never hugged a girl in my life before—but my dick and I were both confused. One part of me was telling myself that this wasn't about sex; rather, it was about our newfound sense of connection and honest conversation.

Since Cassie and I weren't focused on being close, we hadn't been friendly or enjoyed spending time together for the past couple of years. Honestly, if we had been on a real summer vacation somewhere with our parents, we would have been more focused on the sights we were seeing and nothing like this would have happened.

Perhaps it wasn't all that horrible to have a "boring" summer.

Even though everything was feeling so strange right now, Cassie drew back from our hug just enough to plant a large kiss on my lips without using her tongue.

"Hey Connor, I believe we should head out as soon as possible so we can order pizza before Dad gets home. However, hasn't this been amazing?"With a smile, she made her way to the stairs. After exiting the pool, we both changed into our perspiring running tops and shorts, leaving our running shoes and everything else to be carried to the next door.

The first thing we did when we got home was toss our sweaty socks and underwear into the laundry basket, and then Cassie quickly undressed and tossed them in too, and there she was naked again, only this time she was walking to the bathroom to rinse off in the shower, and I undressed too, but she had the water running and hadn't even looked back at me, so I decided to wait until she was done before taking a shower myself, though I certainly wouldn't have minded the chance to soap each other up in the shower at this point, and I wasn't sure how she would feel about it..

I walked to my bedroom and sat on the bed waiting for Cassie to finish up; I heard the bathroom door open and then heard Cassie say, "The shower is all yours, Connor." Confusion seemed to be my default state these days.

As Cassie went into her bedroom, I made it to the hallway just in time to view her butt. Disappointed, I showered in the bathroom and returned to my bedroom with a towel wrapped around me. I changed into a fresh T-shirt and shorts and went to the kitchen.

"Do you want to call in the pizza?" Cassie asked, waiting there in her brand-new outfit.Maybe we should get an extra-large just in case Dad hasn't had takeout with the office crowd, she inquired.

It was Friday, and while the others were willing to put in a little extra effort, they were eager to get home rather than spend another evening dining on Chinese food, so I ordered an extra-large pizza, which arrived about five minutes before Dad's car rolled up.

Mom wouldn't be home for dinner, but she would probably get home about nine, so Dad was happy that we had ordered enough pizza for him. Mom was having supper with some people who were looking at a house.

They'd completed the part of the project they were working on that allowed them to all unwind for the weekend, so Dad dressed into his best clothes, put out some beers for the three of us, and we ate pizza around the kitchen table.

It felt like old times, and I was relieved that I hadn't made things more complicated in my head by trying to get into the shower with Cassie after dinner. (Well, sort of glad, definitely complicated.) We all went out to the back patio and sat around drinking another round of beers and enjoying the evening, waiting for Mom to get home.

When Mom's car rolled into the driveway at about nine-thirty, she was beaming from her supper with her clients—who had evidently had a lot of drinks—and she went to change into shorts and a top before joining us on the patio.

It was lovely to have everyone together again, like old times, and Cassie and I were having the time of our lives with the whole family on the best day of the summer, with Dad buying us beers like we were grownups and Mom and Dad both feeling good about their jobs.

Dad proposed that maybe we could all take a family trip to the shore the following day; it was about a two-hour drive each way, but if we headed out early, that wouldn't be a problem, and we all enthusiastically agreed. Dad didn't have to go into the office on Saturday, and Mom wasn't going to see her clients again until Sunday.

A little before ten o'clock at night, Mom and Dad decided to call it quits because we had to get up early and, quite honestly, they wanted a little alone time.

Once I let Cassie use the restroom first and waited for her to complete, Cassie and I went back to the kitchen to recycle the beer bottles before heading back to get ready for bed.

After finishing, she knocked on my bedroom door and let herself in. "Connor, good night. Cassie remarked, "Thank you, this was the best day of the entire summer."

"Cassie, that was a wonderful day. Really unique. I'm grateful for everything.

As she made her way back to her bedroom, I went to the bathroom to prepare for bed.

Upon eventually making it to bed, I assumed that my thoughts would revolve about our family night or the early shore excursion, but instead they focused on Cassie, our nude hug, and her final kiss on me. And...

We all got up early the following morning, and after the rest of us showered and dressed, Mom served us eggs, waffles, and coffee. We enjoyed a family breakfast together, and thereafter, we all went to pack our things for the day.

My first thought was that it would be easiest to just put on my bathing suit and wear some shorts over it; I didn't think I would need anything else except maybe an extra T-shirt, a cap, and sunscreen; when Cassie reappeared in the kitchen, I noticed she had made the same choice; she was wearing a T-shirt, but I could see her bikini top underneath; I was hoping that Mom and Dad had also made the same choice so that we wouldn't be stranded searching for bathrooms to change into before we could hit the beach.

We left early, which was fortunate because traffic was fairly heavy and it took us two and a half hours to reach the shore. We parked in a large lot near the beach and carried our belongings to the entry point, where Dad had brought some beach chairs for us, which would make our time there much more comfortable.

We had also packed a cooler with some food and water bottles, so we were fairly well-prepared.

Clear and sunny with just enough shore breeze to keep things from getting too hot, the beach was packed but still allowed plenty of room for people to go into the ocean and play in the waves and all that, Cassie and I ducking waves together while Mom and Dad looked like they were having a great time together, still in good shape and actually getting some swimming in.

If Cassie and I had been left alone to play in the waves together in our underwear, that's the only way it could have been better. I wondered if Cassie thought the same thing.

It was time to pick a restaurant for supper, perhaps around four o'clock; we had a long journey ahead of us, and it would be ideal to avoid the dinner hour traffic.

A family day at the beach ended perfectly when we used Google to find a decent seafood restaurant with a view of the ocean.

I hurried next door to feed the cats, who seemed a little irritated at my late arrival and meowed loudly as I hurried to fill their food bowls; fortunately, their litter box was still in decent condition. By the time we got home that night, we were all tired from the sun, playing in the ocean, and the long drive.

After that, I returned home, where Cassie had taken a brief shower before I showered and went to bed. No sooner had I settled into bed when I heard a knock on the door and Cassie said, "Hey Connor, it was a wonderful day, see you in the morning." Good night.

"Good night," I exclaimed. It was a wonderful day. I wanted to say good night to her, but I was so tired that I just nodded off. See you in the morning.

Sleeping later than normal the following morning, I felt as though I needed it.

As I arrived at the kitchen, Dad was preparing to leave for his office, knowing that his team wouldn't be there, but he wanted to organize a bunch of stuff in preparation for Monday. Mom was finishing her coffee, knowing that she would be meeting her first clients at around ten in the morning and that she needed to get to the office early to make sure she had everything she needed, because she had a ton of other house showings scheduled for the remainder of the day. Sunday was a big day for house hunters.

Cassie arrived in time for Dad to say goodbye, and shortly after, Mom left, leaving Cassie and me to prepare breakfast together.

We were just on our own again, and without a car, which felt a little strange. On the one hand, it was a letdown, but on the other hand, I got to spend some quality time with Cassie alone again after our wonderful family day at the coast.

It was nice to have breakfast alone with Cassie, making eggs, toast, and another pot of coffee, but I wasn't sure what we were going to do with the day because we couldn't go on a day trip without a car, and I wasn't sure how things stood in terms of what we had been doing in the pool and how Cassie felt about that after yesterday's family trip to the shore.

We had our second cups of coffee outside on the patio after finishing our eggs and toast, and it was sort of wonderful knowing that we didn't have a long journey ahead of us, so we could relax and enjoy the sunrise together.

What should we do today, in your opinion, Connor?"Cassie queried.

"I'm open to whatever you want," I responded.

I don't think I'm ready for a lengthy jog, though, considering what happened the other day. However, I did enjoy being in the ocean, so I wouldn't mind going back to the pool and swimming more. Perhaps swimming is beginning to become a habit for us."

Head over to the pool in the brightest light of day, with almost the entire day ahead of us? My mind was racing, picturing Cassie getting naked in front of me and us both in the pool with all the time we wanted, and I wouldn't have dared to suggest something like this.

Cassie grabbed my coffee cup for me and we headed to the sink to rinse them before coming into the kitchen.

I couldn't leave things alone, of course. I couldn't let my fantasy come true under my watch.

"Do we need to wear our swimsuits over there?As I asked, I was cursing myself for being such an idiot as I spoke.

"I'll tell you what, I'm going to be bringing a bag with some towels for us," Cassie said as she was rinsing our coffee cups under the faucet without even looking back. We can also pack our suits in the luggage and decide when we arrive."

After pulling out one of her beach bags, Cassie stuffed a few towels inside, tossed in our bathing suits, a few bottles of water from the refrigerator, and a container of sunscreen.

After pulling on our flip flops, we went next door to see how the cats were doing. I gave them some fresh water and food, but I also wanted to remember to give them extra later because this was a bit of an out-of-the-ordinary situation. I looked in the litter box and saw that the poop bag was full, so I had to change it at last, thankfully not too difficult because it was already sealed.

Cassie and I then made our way back to the pool.

When we arrived, Cassie placed the bag on a shaded lounge chair and turned to face me, kicking off her flip flops before reaching down and tossing her top over her head, dumping it onto the lounge chair (not that she was wearing a bra). Later, as I stood there gaping, she removed her shorts, but this time she didn't wear panties.

Naked as she was, she stood there and gazed at me.

"Well," she said, "what are your thoughts?" Would you like me to change into my bathing suit?"

"Oh no, no need at all. Zero necessity. We're alone here.

She just waited for me to take off my clothes too, so I kicked off my flip flops and then took off my T-shirt, throwing it onto the next lounge chair. I was nervous to take off my shorts, even though my dick was already making a tent in them, but I knew that if I didn't take them off, this whole thing would end, and I really didn't want that. I unzipped and undid the button on my shorts, then took them off and threw them over my T-shirt, since I wasn't wearing any underwear today.

You know I like to stare at your boner, Connor, so Cassie stood there inspecting my boner. That is intriguing. I kind of wish I could view it constantly. Additionally, I am aware that you enjoy admiring my pussy and boobs. If you didn't enjoy looking at them, I would be concerned about you. Well, let's just kick back and enjoy our time together while we're nude. You are free to gaze as much as you like, and I am free to gaze as much as I like. That shouldn't be an embarrassing thing for any of us.

"I mean, you do still like looking at my naked body, don't you? Remember, I like compliments."

"I love looking at you naked," I responded. "You're absolutely gorgeous -- and totally sexy, as is pretty obvious from the state of my dick."

"Well, believe me, you are plenty sexy too, and I adore looking at your dick sticking out like that."

Things were rapidly becoming strange. I mean, I was really enjoying being nude for Cassie and knowing that she was adoringly staring at my dick, so I was really liking seeing her nude. Nevertheless, wasn't everything merely incorrect? What motivated us to carry out this action? But why did it make me feel so attracted to it if it was all that wrong? (I ask that you not respond to that question for me.)

I was starting to wonder what was going to happen next. Would we be able to enter the pool at all?

Cassie moved to embrace me, putting her entire body against me. My cock was pressed up against her bush and I could feel it stuck between us. I was shocked to find my sister's body mashed up against my stiff dick. She chose to give me such a hug, and I couldn't believe it.

She was clearly thrusting her bush up against me and grinding up against me. She released her hold on me and kissed me quickly on the lips, just as I was beginning to fear that things would turn terribly awkward.

"All right, it looks like it's time for us to get in the pool," she grinned.

Feeling quite sexy, I followed her into the swimming pool.

Was I meant to act as like nothing had happened at all, or was I just expected to pretend? That this was all simply a harmless, natural thing?

I wanted so badly to get behind her, reach around and feel her breasts and nipples, then reach down and feel her bush and pussy. That was all I could think about at this moment. My desire was to devour her pussy and suck on her nipples. It seemed as though my thoughts were spiraling out of control.

Cassie was grinning at me when I turned to look, acting as though nothing was out of the ordinary.

We did swim for a little while, but it wasn't like we could do any major laps or anything. The pool was pretty little. Then we just kind of relaxed and enjoyed the water while bouncing around in the pool.

My dick had calmed down a little thanks to the swimming. It must have diverted my attention. Still, though...

Subsequently, I observed Cassie approaching the pool's edge and beginning to extract herself. In order to turn around and sit on the edge, she kind of dragged herself up halfway and then began to lean forward to come up even higher. I got to see her pussy for the first time when she managed to spread her legs quite widely while she was doing this. "Connor, can you give me a hand?" she asked to me, still looking like she was having some trouble.

Lend her a hand? I didn't know where to put my hand. Definitely not where I was tempted to put it.

"Just get in between my legs and push me up a little bit further. You can push on my ass if you want to."

I moved between her legs and fixed my gaze on the gap she had left. I reluctantly put my hands on her ass cheeks and gently prodded her up a little. Her ass was incredible. I wanted to just stoop down and give every cheek a deep, full kiss.

She only needed my prodding to raise herself to a slightly higher position so she could turn over and perch on the pool's edge. Her legs ended up on either side of me when she sat there, as I was still standing there. Her sexy lips were there in front of me.

Saying, "Enjoying the view?"

I said, "Oh God, yes." I kind of blurted out what I meant to say, so I'm not sure.

She said, "I'm glad," and spread her legs to let me reach her lips.

I remained motionless, gazing at her ass. I was leaning in to see everything more clearly, I knew that. I was not at all interested in stopping. I just wanted to suck and kiss her pussy and rub my face in her bush.

Looking where I wasn't supposed to, I felt a little bit like a peeping Tom. Cassie, however, was the one who had initiated the encounter and had even spread her legs apart in response to my gaze.

I stood there staring for a little while until Cassie said, "Why don't you hop up here beside me?"

Although I didn't enjoy giving up my opinion, I had to accept what she stated.

Without any help—I'm not sure whether she had actually required any—I managed to get up and flip around to sit next to her, resting my leg against hers.

I was back in full boner mode after spending so much time staring at her pussy, but I made the decision to stop worrying about it.

After we had sat there for a while, Cassie climbed from the ledge and back into the pool, saying, "Okay, my turn." Then, in order to have a better look at my dick, she stepped in front of me and pulled my legs apart. She stared at everything, and I watched as her eyes opened bigger and wider. I was smitten with the way she turned on when she looked at my dick. She continued to draw closer, far closer than I had ever been.

Her words, "I've been waiting for this," "I mean even though it was really beautiful having a family day at the shore yesterday, part of me was just waiting until I could get you naked again. I don't know if you were thinking the same thing."

Yes, I was, I replied.

She stretched out and caressed my balls in her hand, saying, "I love looking at you, Connor. I love looking at your balls, I love looking at your cock, I love seeing how big and hard it is." She said, "Does that feel good?" She bent over and gave them a gentle kiss.

Although I had enjoyed it when she had kissed me on the lips in the past, there was something entirely different about feeling her soft lips kiss my balls. I said, "That feels really good." "I love it."

She continued to lick my balls before moving her lips up my shaft. I was observing her from below. She gently worked her way up to my head to plant a kiss, which not only looked very romantic but also felt amazing. Once she reached the top, she started kissing the top of her head and proceeded to lick it.

"Mmmmm..." She was staring at me. "You taste like chlorine, but I love it. I mean the pool is where all of this started and having both of us naked together and the pool has been the sexiest thing ever."

She continued to lick my cock, descending once more to my balls. It was quite sensual to watch her and feel her tongue on my balls. If she carried on like this for much longer, I started to fear that I might not be able to endure.

"I don't know what's come over me, but I just can't stop myself," she stated. "Just looking at your cock standing up like that for me just turns me on like crazy, and I just want to gobble you up."

She began licking her way back up my penis, and when she reached the apex, she gave it a brief kiss before beginning to take it in her mouth. I was astounded. Since that first day in the pool, I mean, I had thoughts about doing things to her, but I never imagined that I would wind up having her do things to me.

She started to slowly go up and down my cock while encircling my lips around it, taking a little more of me with each kiss. Her lips felt smooth, warm, and seductive. The fact that everything was visible to me and that this was taking place in broad daylight was fantastic. Not only was this a blowjob, in fact my first blowjob ever, but my gorgeous sister was the one pulling it off. Naturally, I wanted to see everything because I didn't want to miss anything. I desired to permanently store all of it in my memory.

I found myself growing more and more attracted to Cassie as she continued. I could sense my own body preparing to arrive.

I didn't want her to stop, but I also didn't want to frighten or disgust her, so I said, "Cassie, I'm going to come. You can stop if you don't want me to come in your mouth." All of that would be ruined.

Rather than pausing or responding, she began to move more quickly over my cock, engulfing more and more of me in her mouth. She continued to suck on me and raised her hand to cup my balls.

It was that. Everything tensed in my body, and I launched myself into her warm, velvety mouth with all of my might. She continued to suck as quickly as she could, and I could see that she was taking in everything I was giving her. Even after I finished, she continued to softly suck and run her tongue over the tip in an attempt to obtain the last bit of fluid.

My cock started to shrink and soften. Cassie continued to grab my balls in her fingers and to hold me in her mouth.

At last, she released my cock from her mouth, bent over, put her arms around my waist, and gave me a hug.

She stared up at me as she finally released her grip. She appeared to be crying. I said, "What's wrong, Cassie?" "Did I do something wrong?"

"No," she responded. "I know it's supposed to be horribly wrong, but it was all so perfect. I loved having you in my mouth and sucking on you, and I loved having you shoot everything for me. You didn't do anything wrong; I'm just crying because it was so beautiful and because I love you so much."

"Maybe it's because it took us so long to get around to this that I'm just a bit depressed. By now, we might have completed this so many times."

I leaped from the pool's edge and stood next to her in the water, giving her a firm hug and a full face of kisses. "I love you too, Cassie," I said. The most exquisite moment of my life was that one. Everything about it. Nothing could have been more ideal. We're more than making up for lost time, in my opinion.

She grinned as she gave me a look. "Really?"You weren't grossed out or anything?" she asked."

I said, "Absolutely not," and I leaned forward to give her a real kiss for the first time, knowing that we had been waiting for this opportunity. I loved the way our tongues played together, the way her lips felt, and the way her mouth felt. She was the ideal kisser.

After a protracted kiss, I released her and declared, "Now it's my turn."

Cassie spun around, hauling herself up onto the ledge and turning to face me, opening her legs wide to allow me to close in.

I lowered my head and gave her another kiss, then I moved it down and started to kiss her breasts and suck on her nipples, enjoying the way her breasts felt full and soft, even though her nipples were now protruding. I also enjoyed playing with her nipples with my tongue, pressing them in as I sucked on her breast, and I felt like I could have done this all afternoon.

Cassie was saying, "Oh God, Connor, that feels so good!" the entire time. It has a lovely feeling!"

I started kissing and licking my way down between her legs, not finished with her breasts, but knowing there would be plenty of time for more of that later. When I reached her bush, I just started rubbing my face against it, loving the whole feel of everything. "That's beautiful, Connor," she was saying. "I love having you do that."

"Cassie, I adore your bush. I adore how it feels on my

face."

Do you think I should shave my pussy? If you wanted me to, I would do that for you. I would do anything to make you feel attracted to me."

"Right now, I love your bush," I replied. "I love you the way you are."

I started to move down her mound, kissing all over it, then I put my lips on either side of her outer lips and sucked and kissed my way down, and then I made my way back up, feeling and tasting her, loving the sensation of her juice on my face and tasting her pussy, and kissing and licking my way all over again.

Cassie was getting more and more fired on, so I went back down to the bottom and inserted my tongue as far as I could reach into her, felt within her, and played with her.

"Connor, I'm very sorry. I'm becoming so hot for you. It feels wonderful. Additionally, I enjoy watching you play with my tongue down there."

I kissed my way back up till I reached her mound once more. By this time, her clit was protruding and it was ready for me. I began playing with my tongue and sucking on her clit.

"Well, that's it, exactly! That is ideal! Continue doing so!Her hips were pressing against my face as she moaned, saying, "Put your finger in me! I want you to be inside of me!"

I continued to suck on her clit as I put my finger into her and saw it glide in and out, dripping with her juice.

When I looked up, I noticed Cassie's tits and I wanted to suck on her nipples again, so I raised my head up to her breasts and started sucking frantically on her hard nipples. Cassie was getting more and more worked up, and her hips were slamming against my face.

"Connor, it feels like the best thing ever. Do with me as

you please! Anything at all!"

I slid back down and started sucking on her clit again, seeing my finger go in and out of her and loving the way her flesh was clinging onto my finger the entire time. I liked sucking on her tits and on her nipples again, but I knew her clit was still waiting for me.

"Oh my goodness, Connor, I'm really sexy. I get so hot for you! I'll be right over to get you!"

I continued sucking and putting my finger in and out of her pussy as I felt her hips move even more quickly and forcefully on my face.

"Connor, I'm coming for you, my God! I'm coming right after you! I adore you a lot! Anything for you, I'll do!"

She continued rushing at me fiercely, and all of a sudden, her hips started moving even faster and slamming into my face, and I felt her juice getting all over my face and heard her cry out, "Oh my God, yes, yes, yes! I'm heading your way! Entire distance!"

I couldn't believe how great it all was, how much I loved her, and I was experiencing the most exhilarating thing I had ever felt in my life—holding onto her hips and forcing my face into her pussy.

Cassie's hips finally stopped moving and she loosened up against me, kissing the top of my head and cuddling me till I glanced up at her again.

She stopped after a while, climbed down into the water next to me, gave me a hug, and said, "It's probably time for us to get outside and put on some sunscreen." We're a little late for that.

"Why don't you spray me with sunscreen to start," Cassie suggested as we emerged from the water and made our way back to the lounge chairs, where she had placed the bag containing the swimming suits and towels.

I took the sunscreen container and sprayed all over her,

rubbing it in afterward, starting with her neck and shoulders, then down to her back, then down to her butt and legs.

One of our smartphones rang as I was working on it, and Cassie checked to see that her phone was ringing.

After taking a few minutes to answer, she said, "That sounds terrific, Mom. When are you coming over to get us? We may be ready really fast because we're right next door to the pool. Two o'clock seemed ideal."

After hanging up, she turned to face me and said, "Oh sh*t. Mom was that. She wanted to know whether we would like to go to the movies with her and then have dinner at a nice restaurant because she had to cancel her appointment for today afternoon. There didn't seem to be a way out. She obviously had a great time on our family day yesterday, and because she had some free time this afternoon, she decided she would like to spend time with us once more. I was unable to come up with any justification."

It would be lovely to do something with Mom on a Sunday afternoon, and although we were both disappointed, there was nothing we could do about it.

"Connor, I've never seen anything as beautiful or sexy as what we just did. I enjoyed getting you to come after me in my mouth and sucking on you. I also enjoyed being consumed by you in that way and being forced to pursue you.

It's not today, but don't worry, I still love your dick and I still want it in me, all the way up to the balls. I want to feel you shooting all your come inside me until it drips out of my pussy. You know I want you to fuck me. I want to feel your dick inside me. But we have time. And it would be nice to do something for Mom, and I think we will enjoy it.

"I should really give you a sunscreen spray before we head

to the house to get dressed. Given how much sun we've had, perhaps this will be somewhat beneficial.

Cassie laid me down on the lounge chair and sprayed me with sunscreen, making sure to get all over my butt and reach all the way up to my cock. After that, we both put on our T-shirts and shorts, and she said, "Hang on a minute."

"It doesn't hurt to cover all the bases," she remarked, "so it's actually a good thing we ended up bringing them with us." She removed our swimsuits from the bag and threw them into the water before squeezing them to dry them slightly.

We put on our flip flops and headed out, with me stopping briefly to go back inside and give the kitties a bit extra food because I knew their routine was truly going haywire.

Upon arriving home, I let Cassie have a shower first. After she finished, I showered and we changed into our regular shorts and T-shirts to accompany Mom to the movie.

A few minutes after we had both made our way into the kitchen, Mom arrived, beaming with anticipation at the prospect of spending a great afternoon with us.

We all went to the movie theater, which was one of those megaplex deals with about 12 different movies showing, giving us at least a reasonable shot at having a movie we wanted to see at the right time; she went back to her room to change into something less formal, and luckily, a new thriller was coming up about in about 15 minutes, so we got tickets and headed in.

There were periods during the movie when Cassie and I could hold hands, and then occasionally Cassie would reach down to feel my crotch. I'm not sure whether Mom expected me and Cassie to sit on either side of her, but I let Cassie sit beside her and then I sat beside Cassie.

We were all a little distracted, but the action packed movie made up for it, and afterward Mom brought us to a fancy steakhouse for dinner; she had contacted Dad immediately after the movie, so he could come too.

We had a great day together as a family, and the food was great as well. Cassie and I realized that because we would both be starting college in the fall, we would need to cherish the times when we could spend as a family.

When we got home, Cassie and I just mentioned that we had fed the neighbors' cats that morning and then jumped into the pool for a quick swim. Dad got out beers for us, and we all went back out to the patio to talk and unwind. We told Dad about the movie, and Mom was able to tell us that her clients were probably going to close on the house she showed them that morning.

It was a lovely evening, and I cherished the sense of family we had while we were together.

Mom and Dad were pretty tired, or maybe just ready for some grown-up time together, after we had talked for a while and finished our beers. Regardless, they got up and kissed us good night before going to bed, and Cassie and I picked up the beer bottles and brought them back to the kitchen to recycle.

It had been a bizarre day, amazing and fantastic, but by now, both Cassie and I were fairly tired.

Cassie proceeded to brush her teeth and do her business first, so I let her go first. After she left for her bedroom, I went to take care of myself.

I returned to my bedroom, got into bed, and put on a midnight T-shirt and some running shorts.

There was a tap on my door, which Cassie answered with a "Good night, Connor." I just wanted to let you know that I had the most amazing day ever today. She hesitated for a second before continuing, "I hope we get to fuck tomorrow. I love you." I want your hot come to fill me up and feel you inside of me."

I answered, "I love you too, Cassie. This was the most amazing day of my life as well. Yes, I want to fuck you all the way and make love to you as well. Everything we've done, I adore."

"Good night, sweet prince." she said as she moved closer to give me a short kiss on the lips before leaving.

There had been a lot of incredible, wonderful, and lovely things that had happened, but I was exhausted and wasn't sure I could take it all in.

I wanted to make sense of everything that had happened that day, but as soon as my head touched the pillow, I dozed out.

The following morning, I arrived as Dad and Mom were wrapping up breakfast, and Cassie arrived a short while after.

Dad explained that his team was taking a field trip to see another team of architects from his firm that had been working on a building project here that was somewhat similar to what Dad's team was working on; it would be a couple of hours' drive each way, and after they met with the team and discussed all the problems, they would tour the building's construction site and tour the building itself; they would probably all end up having dinner afterwards, so he probably wouldn't get home until 9:30 or so.

Cassie and I could order dinner in, or if we wanted to wait, Mom could take us out for dinner when she was done with her final showing of the house that she had been discussing with her clients in the morning. After that, she had an open-house showing from 2 to 6. If there were any interested buyers, it might go longer if they wanted to go into detail about possible offers.

It seemed a little bit restrictive, but at least we wouldn't be relying on the car for today, so damn it.

Cassie was still in her long T-shirt and I was still in my

shorts and T-shirt from when we went to bed, so we decided to cook breakfast first before bothering to take a shower or anything.

After preparing coffee, toast, and eggs for breakfast, we went back outside with our coffee cups to enjoy the morning sun.

We didn't say much, and I felt a little uncomfortable, wondering what the day would hold in light of yesterday's events and the question of whether Cassie was still feeling the same way she had last night.

At last, Cassie stood up, grabbed my cup, and walked back to the kitchen to place them in the dishwasher with the other breakfast dishes.

When she returned, I was standing there ready for her to say, "Hey Connor, I'm going to go take a shower." Would my handsome brother like to come along? Everything is open.

It had been difficult to consider anything else, so it went without saying that I wanted to follow her. However, I also understood there was a dilemma.

"I know it's awkward to discuss, Cassie, but I... I'm not carrying any condoms. Before, I had never truly required any, so... Although the drugstore is not really walkable and we currently don't have a car, I had been thinking I could go there this morning. All I wanted to do was tell you right now. I suppose I simply wasn't planning ahead."

Connor, genuinely? And now you're telling me this? I assume you won't be getting a shower this morning."

I was an idiot, and I couldn't see how this could be fixed. Maybe I should phone an Uber? Oh my God, I couldn't believe this was happening.

"Connor, I was just kidding," Cassie smiled, noticing how dejected I was looking. ripping off your link. Put it out of your mind. It's not an issue. My doctor advised me to start taking the pill when I saw her in the spring since she was aware that I would be attending college in the autumn. She said that although it helps regularize periods, females sometimes make poor decisions in college and she didn't want any of her female patients to have to worry about getting pregnant on top of everything else. I've been taking the pill for some time now. To be really honest, I would detest having to use condoms. Too close between us for that."

On that one, she had undoubtedly played with my mind. I was certain that I had made a huge mistake. I was still experiencing a mild case of shell shock. I don't think I would have survived if she had laughed at my situation, but instead she was just grinning broadly.

"Well, in that case, there is nothing I would love more than to shower with my beautiful and sexy sister."

Leading the way inside the restroom was Cassie. She

crossed the room, opened the shower door, and let the water warm up. She then faced me once more.

"Connor, I have a very important question for you to answer. Are you prepared for this?

"As far as most people are concerned, you are aware that what we did yesterday went way over the line. You are aware that I adored it as well, and I have no doubt that you did too. Not that Mom and Dad would have accepted that as an excuse if they had known, but at least we still had the half-argument that we didn't really do it, we didn't actually have sex. Maybe we could have used it for our own benefit.

"This time is different. There are no excuses. This is weird, and we would be violating one of the biggest taboos there is, and if anyone found out we'd both be totally screwed, probably for the rest of our lives. And I don't want to end up with my brother feeling freaked out or guilty or anything else. I would rather stop now than have that happen."

Give up now? I thought for the first time that maybe Cassie was going to end this whole affair we had been waiting for, and she was watching me. Why on earth was she telling me all of this? I was not bothered at all. If facing the Inquisition meant having the opportunity to finally get my dick all the way inside my twin sister, then I felt like I was ready for it. (Gosh, did I really come across as that sicko?)

"On the other hand," Cassie replied, "I don't want to stop now, and I hope you don't either."

I gave her a look. "Cassie, I love you, and I want you, and I want to be with you and do everything either of us can think of with you. Everything we have done has been beautiful, I don't regret any of it, and I want to keep going until we totally melt into each other. I don't care about the danger for us. The worst thing for me would be to not have you."

Cassie grinned.   I love you too, Connor, and I want to do everything we can think of together. That's so poetic and lovely.

"Now stand there while I take your clothes off, and then you can take mine off."

She stepped forward, grabbed the bottom of my T-shirt with both hands, pulled it up over my head, and I pulled my arms down to allow her to toss it on the ground. She then kneeled down in front of me and started to slowly pull down my shorts, staring intently as my cock emerged—I wasn't quite at half-mast yet, but I was getting there— looking happy to see it again, leaned forward, kissed it, and quickly pulled my shorts down the rest of the way so I could remove them.

After a moment, she stood up and faced me. I reached down with both hands to the bottom of her long T-shirt and started pulling it up, letting her lift her arms to make it easier, but I was taking my time to reveal her boobies and nipples, which were as beautiful as ever. When I finished pulling her shirt over her head, she pulled her arms out, and I let it drop on top of my T-shirt and shorts. Next, I kneeled down in front of her and started slowly revealing her bush and her pussy lips. I moved my head forward to give her bush a quick kiss before I finished pulling her panties down and let her kick them off.

Reaching in to feel the water, Cassie turned back to the shower and said, "Feels perfect, nice and warm and waiting for us."

She entered the shower and guided me in by holding my hand.

As soon as we were standing there in the shower together, she pulled me in close to her and we started kissing. It felt amazing to have our bodies just pressed together, the water streaming down our backs, as we ran our hands over each other's drenched bodies and played with our tongues.

When Cassie finally withdrew, she said, "I guess it's time to start actually washing each other." She took a bottle of body wash with a mint flavor and squeezed some into both of our hands. She then told me to turn around and started rubbing the body wash over my back, down my butt, and between my butt cheeks, definitely pausing to play with my butt-hole along the way. Then she turned me around so she could soap up my front, starting with my chest and moving fairly quickly until she reached my cock and balls, spending a significant amount of time wrapping her soapy hand around my cock and running it around my balls. The mint flavor of the body wash was slightly tingly, which added to the whole experience.

"Connor," she replied, "are you sure that my ass needs that much washing?" She turned around and I began to soap her back, but I ended up spending most of my time toying with it and dragging my finger down from her ass towards her pussy."

"Maybe it doesn't, but I do," I answered.

She pivoted to allow me to launder her front. I spent a good deal of time on her breasts, feeling her nipples harden as I worked. Next, I worked my way down, soaping up her bush, then moving down to her pussy, where I started playing with her clit and running my soapy hand all over it. Her hips started to twitch.

"That feels good, Connor...too good," she replied. "Maybe it's time to start rinsing off the soap."

To ensure that no soap residue remained on our bodies, we alternated between spinning around under the shower and letting the water run off our bodies.

I stood staring at Cassie's incredible butt for a while until she turned to face me again so I could see whether there was any soap left.

I put my hands on her butt cheeks first, and then for some

reason I felt the need to kneel down and kiss her, feeling the water trickle down everywhere as I did so. I pulled her butt cheeks open to see her ass and her asshole, and when I saw that little pink rosebud that the shower had completely cleaned, I leaned forward and started licking all around it, then over it, and finally I started playing with it and sticking my tongue in it.

"What are you doing, Connor? Are you aware of the things you're doing?"

I took a brief break before responding, "Yeah, I know precisely what I'm doing. Your ass is so gorgeous that I had to admit it. Is it upsetting you? I really adore it.

"No, it's pleasant. It is quite pleasant. That turns you on, and I adore that. You are free to continue for as long as you like.

I knew there were other things I wanted to do, even though I did enjoy playing with her asshole with my tongue and feeling everything with it.

I turned her around so her pussy was facing me, put my hands on her hips, rubbed my face in her moist bush, and started playing with her lips with my mouth before nibbling on her clit.

"Connor, would you like me to hurry over to the pool next door and jump in so that I can taste chlorine again?"

"Not necessary. On your own, you taste much better. No chlorine is required. It tastes really good. If we bottled it up, we could become quite wealthy."

Cassie chuckled before realizing again how I was affecting her. "Connor, that feels amazing," she exclaimed. Superior to the swimming pool."

I could feel her hips responding to my actions, which made me feel even better, so I continued to lick, sucke, and rub my face against her pussy. I liked it all.

"Okay, Connor, I'm totally turned on, but now I need my

turn."

I was only semi-hard, but now I felt myself getting completely hard and completely turned on. Cassie pulled me to my feet, and then she kneeled down in front of me and started kissing my cock and my balls. She kissed her way up to the tip of my cock, then took me in her mouth and started sucking.

I had planned to wait, but in these circumstances, waiting was not an option. She put her hands on my ass cheeks and started taking more and more of me into her mouth. Very quickly, I felt my balls and my cock clench, and then all of a sudden, I was spewing everything into Cassie's waiting mouth.

Cassie was consuming everything as I approached her once more, and it was breathtaking to see her do it all. Nevertheless...

"Cassie, that was so wonderful. Oh my god. However, I

had intended to hold off until... I didn't know exactly what else to say."

"Connor, I knew that," she remarked, "but I think I just wanted to ease the tension a little." You won't have any problems becoming hard again, in my opinion."

After we dried off from the shower, Cassie grabbed my hand and walked me back to her bedroom.

"I don't suppose the lounge chairs are designed for this kind of activity, but I had been thinking we could walk next door and be outside in the sunshine and everything. I really don't want to attempt using Mom and Dad's bed, even if I wish my bed wasn't simply a single. That would be excessively strange. In any case, I don't anticipate any issues."

"I love you, Connor, and I want you," Cassie said as she turned to face me in her bedroom. She walked forward, wrapped her arms around me, and planted a kiss on my lips. I want to have sex with you."

"Cassie, I adore you as well. And you are the one person I would really rather make love to. I want to spend every moment with you."

I got on the bed, my knees between Cassie's legs, keeping myself up with my arms, and she lay down with her legs spread wide.

Her nipples were firm and protruded eagerly as I played with them, so I began by kissing her on the lips, then moved down to kiss her all over her neck and finally down to her breasts, where I started by kissing and sucking on each one.

I then moved down, kissing my way down her stomach to her bush, rubbed my face all over her bush, kissed it, and moved down to her mound, kissing it, licking it, running my tongue all over it, sucking on it, and tasting her. She was already wet, and I could feel her hips responding as I ran my tongue between her lips and then inserted it as far as I could, playing with her, tasting her, feeling her juice all over my face.

"Connor, yes, yes, yes! I'm all set! Now, I want you inside of me!"

I leaned forward, lifted my head, and gave her another kiss on the lips. Then, I guided my cock to her opening, rubbing it up and down between her lips as she spread her legs and pushed her hips up toward me. I watched as my cock entered her, feeling the walls of her pussy begin to wrap around it. I moved slowly, appreciating that her shower blowjob had prevented me from being agitated or hurried. I pushed in slow thrusts, pulling back a little before pushing further in again.

"Connor, you make me feel so good inside! Oh my God!" I want you to be everything to me!"

"Cassie, you feel fantastic. I adore how you feel around by

my cock. It has a lovely feel."

I thrust harder and faster, and soon I felt myself all the way within her with my balls resting against her. Her pussy felt extremely tight as I continued, but by now she was reaching out and holding the cheeks of my ass to help pull me into her.

I took a minute to allow it sink in for both of us. "Cassie, every single part of me is inside of you. You feel so wonderful, and I cherish you."

"Connor, I adore you and the way you feel inside of me. I want to feel you fucking me hard right now. I want to feel like you're about to shoot straight through me!"

I started to move harder and quicker, and her hips hammered against my body as we moved in unison.

I attempted to turn off some of the feeling in my cock so I could last longer, pausing briefly as I pulled out before thrusting again since I didn't want it to end just yet.

I enjoyed seeing her on top of me, allowing her take charge, and letting her lean forward so I could suck on her breasts and nipples while we kept on fucking. I decided to switch up what we were doing, and I signaled for her to help us both flip over so she would be on time.

"Connor, this is really great. This is amazing. Are you fond of it? It feels incredible.

I adore it. I adore being able to feel everything you're doing to me just by staring at you like this, Cassie."

She was examining her range of motion, bending forward, bending back, and spinning sideways. "I had no idea that I would be able to do all these different things," she said.

I was able to hang on a bit longer this way, but even after taking a shower, I could still feel my endgame coming on.

"Cassie, let's flip back over. I'm preparing to arrive."

I could have come with her riding me, but I wanted the opportunity to pound her as hard as I could to finish up, so we flipped over so I was on top again.

I was fucking her as hard as I could, my hips beating harder and faster against her.

"Connor, oh my god, absolutely! Give me as much fuck as you can! Approach me! I want you to shoot all of your energy into me!"

I started to come in harder than I had ever come in before, wanting to fill her up with all of me, feeling my body exploding inside her and her hips pressing against me even more quickly.

I'll be there, Connor! It's really pleasant! I cherish you!"

It felt great, our hips grinding together as we both came.

We were in a place that neither of us could have imagined even a week ago, and we had no idea what kind of complications there were going to be. I lowered my body onto her and hugged her tightly, and she held me tight too. Neither of us said anything, overwhelmed by what had just happened -- and maybe also by what we had just done.

At last, I moved away from Cassie and lay down next to her, our hands clasped.

"What state are you in?I questioned her.

She exclaimed, "I'm feeling amazing. That was the most exquisite experience of my life. I had some soreness, but nothing serious. Definitely worthwhile. You were bigger than I had imagined, and feeling you inside of me was an entirely new experience even though I had stuck my fingers in there quite a bit during the previous few years.

"You know I've talked to some girls who lost their virginities to guys who just wanted them as trophies. Once the guys had had sex with them, they didn't care anymore. They lost their trophy value. It wasn't that those girls didn't like sex -- later on they found guys who really cared about them and sex was wonderful -- but they felt lousy about the way things had gone that first time. It's not like that at all for me. This was perfect. And I have a feeling it's going to keep on getting better."

"It was flawless," I declared. "It couldn't have been any better. I guess there's something to be said for violating taboos. In no way I am going to stop loving you, ever."

Cassie grinned. We resumed our kissing and simply holding hands.

My cock was thinking about getting hard again as I was giving her a hug while we were still both nude. Cassie could feel it certainly increasing a little.

You're pretty huge, and that was quite the introduction to sex, so I think it might be a good idea to take a break. My pussy might want a little bit of recovery time." "I'm pleased you're ready for more," she added.

"Perhaps we ought to go feed the kitties and go in the pool?"

"That sounds good," I replied. "We have a long afternoon

ahead of us."

"I think it's a good idea to have wet suits when we come back from the pool," Cassie commented as we got up and showered. After changing into our shorts and T-shirts, Cassie packed our suits in the bag with some towels.

After getting some yogurts in the kitchen, we went to the next room.

I entered the front door of the neighbors and saw the cats running around, leading the way into the kitchen and meowing for food; I fed them and checked on the litter box, which was still fine for the time being, and Cassie and I headed back outside to the pool.

The pool appeared flawless as usual, but I was unable to process how much had changed since our previous visit.

It didn't seem nearly as big of an issue this time, and I didn't even have a boner; maybe it was because I'd previously been here before, but it was also because I felt so much more at ease with Cassie.

"I guess I never saw you before when you didn't have a boner," Cassie said, glancing at me after I had settled my shorts into one of the lounge chairs. "It's neat seeing it just hanging down and swinging back and forth." I would just like to know how it feels.

"I don't think I ever gave that much thought," I replied. "It's difficult to put into words." I suppose it's just there, and unless anything gets difficult, I don't give it much thought. Then I give it a lot of thought."

"Maybe if I had big floppy tits," Cassie joked, pausing for a while. "Would you like it if my tits were bigger?" she asked. They're not really large or anything."

"Cassie, they are flawless." There's no way I would want them otherwise. I truly do adore them exactly the way they are, but I guess I would be okay if they were different. I'm not a huge fan of big breasts."

We descended the stairs into the pool, which felt ideal. We stood there unwinding for a while, and then attempted a few lengths of swimming; it was far too small for serious laps, but even that little workout felt fantastic, and we would probably have to start running again soon.

We heard a cell phone ring as Cassie was approaching me. "I think that's my phone," she remarked, "but I should check it in case it's Mom or Dad."

I heard her say, "Oh, hi Mom," as she leaped out of the water as quickly as she could and made it to the phone before it stopped ringing. Where are you? Oh, I see. Yes, suit up and come hang out with us. We'll be present.

After closing the conversation, Cassie rushed to the towel bag, took out her swimsuit, threw mine to me, hurriedly put her own on, and came down the stairs to join me in the pool.

"Mom's at home," she informed me, adding that although

the meeting with the clients concluded earlier than she had anticipated, she doesn't open her house until two. When she returned home to check on us, she reasoned that we may be over here and decided to try my phone. She reasoned that she had ample time to visit and swim with us before she had to go for her open house.

That would have been so much better. Would we still be in bed if Cassie hadn't been sore? Would we have gone to the neighbors' pool without our suits? In any case, we were both wearing our suits and looked like a typical brother and sister.

And sure enough, ten minutes or so later, Mom showed there, looking very happy about getting to have a cool dip in the pool with us on a hot day, and sporting a cover-up over her bathing suit.

Mom looked happy as she kicked off her flip flops, removed her shawl, and came down the steps into the pool to join us.

I'm overjoyed that I was able to join you and view the pool. The closing proceeded well and quickly, giving me plenty of time before I had to spend the remainder of the afternoon in an open house. How much time have you two spent here?"

"Oh, a little while," Cassie replied. "We just hung out for a while after having a leisurely breakfast and coffee outside on the patio." However, we were itching to return to the pool and tend to the kitties. Isn't that a pretty lovely pool?"

"It's amazing," Mom exclaimed. "We might be able to get one for our backyard if your Dad's project turns out really well. In warm weather, it would be really fantastic."

Naturally, Cassie and I had not planned for Mom to be a part of our day, so there was a slight awkwardness to the whole thing. We couldn't be angry with Mom though, because she was having so much fun with us here at the pool.

Mom commented, "This is really lovely, and I'm so glad I got to join you here," after about thirty minutes. However, I have an open house starting at two, so I suppose I should return home, get ready, and go over there to make sure everything is set up. Officially, the open house ends at six, but occasionally, people stay a bit later. If you feel like waiting, you kids can order takeout, but if not, let's all go out to eat and celebrate my house closing. When I'm finished, I'll give you a call to find out what you want to do."

Mom went back up the pool stairs, put on her flip flops and wrap, and walked back to the next door.

We both let out a sigh of relief, Cassie and me. There were other ways that things could have turned out far worse. What if she had returned while we were still in bed, perhaps even during our sexual encounters? That would have been terrible and the worst-case situation. It served as a warning to us both about the dangers we were assuming.

However, what if Mom had just chosen to go next door without warning and we had been "skinny-dipping" together while we were in the pool? It's awkward, but not nearly as horrible. It was probably something she would have brought up to Dad, and they would have talked and worked things out together.

(She might have seen us doing more than just skinny-dipping, of course. Let's avoid even considering that idea.)

It served as a clear reminder to treat everything with seriousness. We weren't interested in stopping, but we also weren't interested in being discovered.

Cassie and I waited in the swimming pool. Although Cassie had grabbed my hand in hers, we were obviously not going to take any chances that the other day would happen again.

Everything had become quiet. We were both too scared to breathe.

We heard our front door close, followed shortly after by Mom's car starting and driving gone, after what seemed like the longest wait of my life. I gave Cassie a quick glance and we exchanged hugs.

This whole situation may have served as a chastisement, but for some reason it didn't appear to.

I said, "Alright, Cassie." "Open house is scheduled for four hours. Dad is out of town, therefore she needs to be there the entire time. Come with me.

Cassie and I only needed to change into our bathing suits this time, so we could return home. We simply threw our T-shirts and shorts in the towel bag, hurriedly dried ourselves, and returned to our apartment.

After going to the bathroom, we undressed her suits and hung them up on the shower rack.

Cassie asked, "Do we want to rinse off the chlorine?"

Chlorine is sexy, no way. We'll both become excited about it. Do you think you could handle one more round?"

"Although I still have some pain, I'm more lustful for you than I am sore. Right now, I want to fuck you again."

"Let's use my bedroom this time," I replied. "I want to have memories of us fucking when I'm in bed tonight."

We pressed our nude bodies together as I drew her to me and planted a kiss on her. We then made our way to my bedroom.

"I want to start out on top this time," she stated.

I dropped onto the bed. She took my cock in her hand, sat down next to me, and started sucking on me. I had been feeling a little down after all that with Mom, but as soon as I was in Cassie's warm, velvety tongue, I became very rigid. As she was sucking on me, I reached out to feel her breasts and felt her nipples harden. I started stroking her back and legs as I continued to observe her.

I finally said, "Okay," after a short period. "If you keep going, we're going to have a long wait before I'm ready again."

After a moment, Cassie sat up. Subsequently, she straddled me on the bed.

"Why don't you start by moving up and sitting on my face first?" said I.

She lowered her pussy onto my face as she proceeded up. I cherished this brand-new chance. I started playing with her, kissing her, licking her, and sucking her. I was playing with her, moving my tongue between her lips and then putting it inside. She tasted very good, and I enjoyed getting her juice all over my face. I raised my face again after that. I started sucking on her protruding clit and playing with it with my tongue. Her hips were firmly pressing up against my face.

"Connor, I adore that," she exclaimed. "Do you like it?"

"I absolutely love it, I love feeling your pussy all over my face, and feeling how wet and turned on you are."

She declared, "I am ready."

Her pussy was over my cock when she descended again. She grasped my cock, pressed it against her pussy, and started to slide down on it. "Connor, you feel amazing. I adore having this kind of control."

I watched as she moved slowly up and down my cock, causing it to get moist and shine with her juice. She became increasingly aroused the further she got into my cock, and before long, she forced her way down till I was entirely inside of her.

"Connor, do you like that? Am I feeling well? I adore writing you in this manner and adore having you inside of me."

"Cassie, you feel incredible. You feel flawless. This is really lovely."

Cassie continued to ride me, swaying back and forth, bending forward occasionally so I could suck on her nipples and kiss her breasts.

"Would you like us to try doggy-style?" I said after a time.

"Sure, that sounds like fun." She might not have understood what doggy-style meant exactly, but she was game for anything.

I managed to convince her to move away from me long enough for me to escape beneath her. Then, as I moved behind her, I instructed her to bend forward on her hands and elbows. I began massaging my cock over her pussy when she leaned forward in that manner and pointed up at me. I then started to gently push it in.

"Connor, wow. This is really dissimilar. It has a distinct

feel. It's seductive in a whole new sense."

I kept going in and out while observing how wet her pussy made my dick look. While I was fucking her, I was also savoring the sight of her ass and asshole. For an instant, I bent forward to caress her breasts and play with her nipples, but then I straightened up, grasped her ass cheeks, and started rubbing my thumb inside, getting closer and closer to her rosebud. After a while, I began to play with her by popping her rosebud open and putting my thumb inside.

"That's quite kinky, Connor. It's kind of sultry, but I guess I wasn't prepared for it. But keep going. This is about the least kinky thing we should be concerned about, given what we're doing in the first place."

I continued to play with her ass, slipping one or the other in even deeper and massaging her rosebud with both thumbs. Observing my cock enter and exit her pussy and feeling her reaction to what I was doing to her ass made me realize that I couldn't hold on much longer.

"Cassie, I'm coming; I'm coming for you all the way." I simply want you to know how much you make me fall in love with you since you're so gorgeous and seductive."

"Connor, fuck me as hard as you can. What you're doing is fantastic. Continue like this so I can accompany you!"

I began to come, blasting everything deep inside her pussy as soon as I felt my balls spasm.

"Connor, I will be joining you as well! Give me as much fuck as you can! I want to feel your fists hitting me.

We were both coming now. My cock was spurting deep inside Cassie, and I could feel her hips thrusting up against mine. This was such a different kind of experience. I adored that.

When we had both done getting dressed, she collapsed into the bed, and I collapsed onto top of her. We slept there for a little while, her head turning and me kissing her cheek.

After that, I rolled off of her, she rolled over, and we just lay next to each other.

"It was incredible," she exclaimed. "Especially with you toying with my ass, it was really unusual. I adored that.

"I really enjoyed it. I want to use every method possible to make love to you."

After exchanging kisses, we walked back together while holding hands.

Cassie added, "I'm also happy we fucked in both beds." "That way, both of us can feel the memories tonight when we're in bed."

"It would be nice if we could be in the same bed tonight," I said. "But still, this is been the most perfect and beautiful day of my life."

"Mine too," replied Cassie.

Cassie remarked after a short period, "Do you know a lot more positions? Perhaps we ought to locate a book, such as the Kama Sutra or something similar? Perhaps turn it into a project so you can experiment with different things?"

"Maybe," I replied, "but I really enjoy what we're doing right now." As of right now, I have no problem continuing with our current course of action."

Cassie eventually sat up. "I have to go urinate," she stated. "I really enjoyed what we just accomplished, but I'm hurting a lot again. I don't believe I'm prepared for another round at this time.

I got it. It had been the ideal first day of sex. And summer still had a long way to go. I waited for Cassie to exit the restroom before using the restroom.

I got out, and we both changed into clean T-shirts and shorts before going outside to the patio.

"Did you want to order take-out, or wait and see when Mom is ready to take us out to dinner with her?"

"I believe we ought to wait for Mom. Not only would she probably take us to a fantastic steak restaurant, but I know she would truly like that. After today, I believe I could use a steak."

LOL, said Cassie. "I agree, it would be nice to let Mom take us out to dinner."

We sat there, and Cassie finally said, "You know, maybe we need to think about where all this is going," after we had been silent for a while. If we exercise caution, we can continue doing this for the remainder of the summer. But what about when we visit State in autumn? Did you realize that trying to get into each other's dorm rooms may grow awkward, or were you considering ending things at that point? which, as far as I'm aware, would make sense."

I knew I didn't want to end it now that she'd brought it up, even if I'd been trying not to think about it too much.

I took a moment to consider it. What would you think if we approached Mom and Dad and proposed that we get a two-bedroom apartment together rather than settling for cramped, noisy dorm rooms? We might say that in this way we could keep an eye on each other to make sure that none of us ended up dating someone unsavoury or got into trouble or anything." We could also study together and prevent one another from slacking off."

Cassie gave me a glance. She was, I believe, quite pleased that I had not wanted to give up and that I had thought of an idea that would work well, if we could convince our parents of it.

"We're going to have to really consider how to present this idea to Mom and Dad after doing some research about housing, apartments, and apartment rentals," she stated. One thing is for sure: if we had a two-bedroom apartment, they would consider it great that we had somewhere to stay when they came to visit."

"That's definitely an argument," I replied. "We have to look at rentals, apartments, and other things. However, it's well worth the try. Naturally, there would also be other issues to resolve. What information would we impart to our classmates and the ones we made friends with? If we told them we were a brother and sister living together in an apartment, would it look suspicious? Or are they just pals with the same last name? distant cousins, perhaps? We may not look exactly alike, with my dirty blonde hair and wavy eyes and your straight dark hair and blue eyes, but our bodies are close enough that I doubt Sherlock Holmes would be required to make a comparison. However, there would be a ton of issues if we announced huge everyone that we were married, particularly when Mom and Dad paid us a visit."

We remained silent for a while longer while we sat there.

Whatever the case, it was going to be complicated. However, living in a dorm would be even more difficult.

Both of us feeling a little intimidated by the intricacies of it all, we sat there and stopped talking.

Cassie said, "You remember how I told you about how my doctor prescribed the pill and how it helped me have more regular periods? I should probably note that my menstruation is supposed to start this Friday. All I wanted was for you to not be taken aback."

"Well," I replied, "that still gives us a few days."

"Connor, it's not the end of the world just because I'm having my period. We are not limited to what we can do; there is at least one more thing we could do. Don't appear so disappointed, then.

Truly? Was it what she said? I had thought about it a little more than that, particularly this afternoon while we were practicing doggie style. I started to question if I could hold off until the weekend.

Cassie and I did nothing except wait for Mom to call while leaning back in our chairs and holding hands.

Acknowledgments

The Glory of this book's success goes to God Almighty and my beautiful Family, Fans, Readers & well-wishers, Customers, and Friends for their endless support and encouragement.

About The Author

I've spent nearly a decade penning romantic novels. As a passionate writer of erotica, I craft dark, romantic erotica. Anime Naked Truth Se of Sacred Sexuality: Forbidden Seducing Short Stories of an Erotica Nude Sexy Girl Poster. Alongside Erotic Mystery Fiction, Victorian Erotica Sex, Black & African American Erotica, Euthanasia, Daddy Teaching, Forced Domination, Alpha Monster Cuckold, and BDSM for Adults, there's an Erotic Fiction in Kinky Family. I write dark, sensual romance because I adore the power of darkness and everything that it entails. Romance novels have always been my favorite kind of books, and now I'm writing them. The idea that you will like reading and enjoying my fiction as much as I enjoy pushing the frontiers of sexual pleasure in my writing thrills me more than anything else.